"I am the dirt of Bethlehem. I am the stretching night sky over Israel. I am the black night of Egypt. The dream to consume is upon us, a light to touch us" Davii continues reading from his novel. He had finished writing it today. He had been struggling with the ending of the poem he had written within it. Its last text stated "There is no light in he, Beyond the sharp autumn leaves is a monster whom death retreats from" This line puzzled him as he does not remember writing it.

AF582705

The pacing of steady footsteps start to get closer to his room door. He puts his pants on quickly before his mother enters the room. “Hey! Good morning, the food is ready downstairs so come eat” his mother said with such energy. Davii with a solemn expression looks towards his novel and simply closes it back. He thinks to revisit it later when he has had some inspiration. He finishes dressing himself and puts his curly brown hair underneath his red hoodie. Davii and his mother leave his room and begin walking downstairs when he notices his older sister’s door is closed still. “Is Cilia coming down this time? It’s been at least a week. His mother replies “Im not sure, she seemed like she was thinking about it the day before yesterday but we need to give her space. Shes been through a lot and its up to us to know when to pry and when to simply be patient with her” They sit around the table and hear a thump come from upstairs. Davii looks to the top of the stairs but is plagued by visions. He believes he sees a person, a black figure walking back and forth from each room. His mother Clara begins walking upstairs to check on the noise. A series of whispers can be heard from the daughter cilia's room. Clara knocks on the door only for the whispers to cease. Cilia opens the door seemingly exhausted. "Hey, are you okay? We heard a loud noise downstairs" She replies to her softly. "I am fine mom, I promise?" she smiles as a drop of black blood begins leaving her nose. She slams the door in her mother's face and the whispers can be heard again, only this time there is the clear distinction between the whispers and the mysterious tampering with the wall. "Is she drawing something? Sweetie let me check your nose I don’t think that color is normal” She opens the door again to discover her daughter has used the blood from numerous animals she assumingly captured to write an indecipherable language on the walls. Symbols and text that her mother could not understand. A couple of the animals still alive try to move or make noise but are seemingly silenced somehow. Her daughter turns back to her and lets out a sinister screeching yell. Davii at the bottom of the stairs jumps up, his hands and legs begin shaking as he can see a black figure standing behind his mother at the same moment; she frighteningly slams the door shut. She begins softly crying as she is frozen in place. She runs back downstairs and simply continues eating. She vomits beside her chair and excuses herself to her room. Davii sits there contemplating. He thinks he has to get away from here. “Mom im going to school ok?” He gets up and goes to retrieve his bag from his room. He looks out the window to see his sister cilia walking with a man in a black suit. He runs downstairs to the front lawn and discovers no one is there and his sister ominously stares at his from the window at her room.

As he walks down the street he meets up with his oldest friend York. A rather tall young man whose stature is more up right compared to him. Surely a symbol of inner confidence. “Yo, didn’t think you were coming today with all that shit going on around here” Davii looks at him confused. “Whats going on at school?” he asked. “Well I heard that someone said that the gym teacher Mr. Eves found a group of students writing crazy shit on the walls of the girls and boys locker rooms. Said after he caught them they tried to kill him or something like that" Davii with a concerned expression gasps softly. "Dude are you fucking serious? No way" he said in disbelief. "Yeah man its true, I seen it on Instagram this morning. Aye I didn't wanna say nothing but someone said they saw your sister there" They are interrupted and bumped by multiple people seemingly fleeing from the school as they turn the corner of the street. Parents are piling up in cars, the traffic is insane. They step through the doors to discover an array of mangled bodies have been strung up inside the school hallways as naked women and men are taken away in handcuffs. The police shove them out and one says "Come on guys, This type of crazy shit shouldn't be an image you remember" The doors close as news teams gather around and begin reporting for multiple different stations.

"We are live from Stacia High as a terrible tragedy has taken place... A group of students were murdered seemingly this morning before the school was supposed to be open. The men and women suspected of this have been arrested as they were still on school grounds when the authorities arrived" The newscaster cannot hide the trembling in her voice. Davii and York begin walking home with another friend who's supposed to meet them at the corner by breakfast. Miranda greets both of them sadly and worried. "Man I'm glad you guys weren't in there!!" she hugs both of them tightly. "Its awful, I was in cheerleading tryouts on the field when everything went down. They said we had to use the new building locker room but I didn't know why. I guess I do now but isn't this crazy? What kind of fucking cult psychos do some shit like this?" she asked, Davii replies "Cult psychos do this type of stuff obviously. Come on let's go get breakfast from Jones Diner up the road" A reporter is seemingly watching York and his friends as he takes multiple pictures of them. They arrive at the diner and can see on the television in the corner that in Allentown PA, at a church multiple individuals killed themselves and multiple others in a religious cult meant to worship what seems to be a brand new deity. "So people are worshipping black lakes and gold men now?" York says as he reads the story on his phone. "Dude you work quick" Miranda said to him. "Gotta be quicker than this is journalism is gonna work out for me.

Davii begins getting a call from his mother. “Davii, hey its mom. Im sorry about this morning but Cilia is gone and were looking for her now. Please come home because a detective needs to speak to us both” davii gets up quickly and begins running home. He accidentally bumps into a man who falls to the ground. He arrives at his house to find four police vehicles out front. He walks through the front door and a detective with his mother greet him with 4 officers present as well. “Mr. Kallister, you mind if I call you davii like your mom?” he asked him with a rather soft voice for a man. ‘No its fine, whats going on? My mom told me I had to be here” The detective steps back and begins talking to davii and his mother. “It would seem cilia was in fact involved in the tragedy at the school, We have her on camera doing some pretty heinous things and we are gonna have to arrest her. I came to say my hands are tied and I'm going to try my best to get her into a good rehabilitation center" He is interrupted by Davii. "Today..she scared our mom pretty bad, I understand what you have to do but please don't explain it. I don't think we can take knowing every detail please and we don't need you to explain to us that your going to do your best. If she was involved with that cult then whatever happens probably has to happen" The detectives and the officers begin heading upstairs. Clara goes into her bathroom and davii stays in the kitchen. Cilia can be heard assaulting the officers. They carry her by holding a leg and an arm on each side. She is placed within the car and makes eye contact with Davii before being taken away.

The whispers are now loud in his ear, A cold air surprises him as the hairs on his arm stand up. “I know this was something I wouldn’t wanna go through if I was a dad” Davii checks on his mother. “I’ll be out in a second, I just want to clean off my face. My eyes are so red” She pretends to laugh jokingly but the sobbing is still surfacing. Davii walks up to his room and begins watching tv. The story about the cult is all over the news.

Even on music channels the programming is paused every couple hours or so to give a moment of silence to those who died. Davii closes his eyes to take a quick nap before he has to help with dinner or possibly just cook it himself. As he dreams, he is walking down the street and he notices a black man clad in a black suit with a gold tie standing in front of him at the corner. He looks at him slowly moving his long twisted hair. His eyes were black and gold with the gold of his iris seemingly dipping into the black sclera of his right eye. He begins walking towards Davii with a horrible smile upon his face. A smile that shows not the sinister thoughts of a demon but the joyous expression of someone who is about to claim something they desire. “You, you will be my exodus. Join your madness with mine, your roots with my voice and be suffocated through me” Davii awakes in a cold sweat with the feeling that someone has been gripping his shoulder. Its soreness causes him to wince at the pain when he gets up. He goes downstairs to discover the front door is wide open. He steps out and finds his mother naked on the front lawn speaking in another language before impaling her forehead with a hunting knife. “Holy shit! Mom! Mom!!” neighbors come help but the sound of sirens drowned out conversation or the weeping of davii for his mother’s life.

A fire can be seen from over the houses on the other street. People on fire begin running the other direction with some seemingly injured in other ways. From the around the corner comes a creature of haunting proportions. Its body seemingly the mangled remains of multiple human bodies. It grabs one of the fleeing people and rips off an arm and leg, it then begins eating him from the bottom half up. The man screaming for help but his words are drowned out by the sounds of chaos and blood gushing from his mouth. The creature turns its head to davii and his neighbors and begins a terrifying walk their way, as it got closer it seemed to be at least 10-13 feet tall. Its multiple limbs seemingly working in unison to produce its haunting posture. Davii begins sprinting in the other direction and tries to call York and Miranda. Miranda answers but asks for Davii's help as she is trapped in the supermarket bathrooms. She has locked the door but can hear something scratching at the door. York answers after and says he will meet him at the corner of jones café, he knows about the large creature and explains that it happened about a couple hours ago at the school. He escaped himself on his dads motorcycle. Davii runs through an alleyway and up a firescape to see York on the roof. He signals him and they maneuver through the chaotic looting and rioting to meet at the corner spoken of. Davii explains to York the situation with miranda. “I think miranda is at the grocery store. She said she was locked behind the bathroom stalls and she locked the door for the bathroom but I don’t know how long she has, she says something has been staking out the door and she can hear it” They look at each other seemingly trembling but begin looking around to see what they can find amidst the chaos.

Across the street they witness a truly frightening display. A man walking in ragged pants and boots with a black hood begins screaming nonsense into the air. His body begins to bulge and grow as four tentacle like appendages rip from his back, his chest explodes into a bloody mess revealing his rib cage and multiple fangs shoot out from the opening. The bottom of his face he rips off revealing a gaping maw leading to the chest opening. His eyes go from brown to red and the hood seems to be fused into his skin now as his arms and legs grow double their original size. York pulls davii behind a car. They sit there quietly as they listen to the cultist begin killing everyone. Davii finds a large hunting knife in the passenger seat of the car and goes to grab it. He puts it in his bag and tells York the plan. “Okay I think if we make a run for it while it deals with the rioters we should be fine but I know about your football injury. I know you cant run as fast so I need you to hold my hand alright? Im gonna slightly pull you as we run but its gonna hurt” York shakes his head in agreement. They begin running down the street luckily unnoticed. As they make their way across the bridge to reach the grocery store on the other side they begin hearing strange noises coming from under the bridge in the dark. Davii pulls the knife out of his bag and York walks slowly behind him. The noises begin getting louder and soon they begin running away from what they hear. As they make their way over the bridge towards the grocery store parking lot. They find that there were suffering from auditory hallucinations. They arrive at the parking lot to find multiple dazed individuals wandering. They are covered in blood, like someone splattered it onto them. York accidentally softly bumps into a shopping cart that causes it to begin rolling. They duck behind a car in the parking lot. Through the window they notice the wandering people have begin converging on the cart like hungry beast. Yelling and roaring into the sky. They begin sniffing around and jumping on numerous cars to check them.

One finds davii and York and attacks them. Davii quickly dispatches it by stabbing it through the mouth before it can roar. The monster begins trying to reach davii past the knife but just falls over instead. It catches the attention of the others and York and davii go under the car to hide. They disperse as a car alarm goes off across the lot. Davii and York make a run for it and end up entering the grocery store and locking the doors.

Inside they can hear other monsters lurking about in the aisles. They walk slowly through the aisles they make sure are empty and head towards the rest room for miranda. There they find one of the monsters has attached itself to the ceiling above and has its eyes closed. They walk towards the bathroom and text miranda to open the door but quietly. The bathroom door begins opening incredibly slowly as miranda who is shaking in fear tries to leave. She reaches davii and York but has a deep scratch on her leg.

"I stopped the bleeding with my shirt, I used it as a tourniquet. Im okay. Just please lets get out of here" The monster opens its eyes and begins making a strange sound. The creature is seemingly wailing or crying but it is drowned by a disgusting gurgling and sinister roaring it cannot help but produce. It detaches from the ceiling destroying multiple aisles showing its sheer size. Davii, York and Miranda begin slowly moving around the creature using the medicine aisle the stretches towards the back door and the pharmacy. They make it over the counter and the massive creature begins looking around. Multiple other infected people come running in making horrible fleshy sounds as they move almost as if something else is forcing their body to move from the inside.

A truck drives straight into the store knocking the infected and the massive creature over. They take this time to escape through the pharmacy back door and leaves the monsters to their fate. A large explosion is seen at the store as one person ablaze walks out, the sound of a man crying for his daughter ceases as the person drops to the ground joining the charred remains of the other bodies. “Come on, that explosion had to have been heard by god knows what” Davii exclaims that he still has his hunting knife. “We should go over there to Best Buy, it doesn’t look too bad over there. We should see if we can find anything in some of these cars or maybe even on a couple bodies” Miranda begins shaking her head. “I cant do that, I cant go around searching dead bodies. That’s just insane” York stops her and says angrily “Wake up! They are not gonna need whatever they have because they are dead, dead as fuck miranda. Unless you want to end up like them I suggest you suck that shit up and hopefully we can find a gun or something better than a couple knives” Davii puts his hand on her shoulder. “hey just stick with us, were gonna be okay. It might be a bit before we can get back on apex but we are fine now so lets try and keep it that way" miranda inhales and exhales a few times and follows closely behind davii.

They begin walking through the shopping center parking lot observing the environment to ensure they know what's coming and what's not. York manages to get the doors to a pickup truck open revealing a sawed off shotgun, a pistol and a multitude of knifes inside of a bag. They are approached by the owner. 'Hey! I don't know who you are but get away from my truck. I need everything I got so spare your words and keep it moving" Davii comes up behind him with the hunting knife. "Please don't do that sir, We just need something to keep going please. We don't want to do this. We aren't criminals" The man lowers his rifle.

“Next time say something like that earlier. I aint got much but I can give you this pistol and some ammo. The man hands them what they need and gets in his truck, he speeds off as his instincts hammer at him. “Well that was just lucky, he could’ve just killed us” York says as he exhales in relief. “Killing three teenagers probably wasn’t on his to do list today York” Miranda jokingly says. The three share a laugh for a few seconds but overhear a notification from their phones. “The phones still work?! Lets see what is really going on here” Davii begins watching the news on his phone. “The latest here at Vox Media, A dangerous cult seems to have taken control over a large portion of the city and have begun indoctrinating members, the national guard has been mobilized and are facing the cult now.

Some have described the situation as "Urban Warfare" as the cult is fighting back in the hundreds of thousands all over the nation. We go to New Haven Virginia to get a closer look at the chaos ensuing" The news broadcast quickly turns to live footage. At least a hundred men and women dressed in black cloaks adorned with a gold trim and a strange series of symbols written all over are marching with blades and assault weapons. They are beginning to overwhelm the military through sheer numbers and ambush. On camera we see multiple cultish bursting into disgusting monstrosities that begin tearing through the military. "Oh my god, help me! Please don't" A soldier says as he is on video being torn limb from limb as he is eaten alive by multiple creatures. The broadcast returns to the newscaster. She stutters a bit when beginning to speak again. “As you can see the nation is in a dire situation and hold on people…im getting information that the federal government will be deploying more military with heavier firepower to combat the situation. Davii’s phone dies abruptly. “This is happening everywhere? For there to be so many it’s a good thing we got away from downtown” Davii, Miranda and York all begin holding their heads and clenching their fist from pain. “Ahhh my head, it feels like its being hit with a hammer” A voice is heard in the back of Davii’s mind. “We, I am many. I have finally come to bring the death that is forever. My hordes will eviscerate every last life until no one but our slaves remain. I will swallow you Davii, you know it. I am coming. You will be my second vessel, my eternal dream. You are chosen and I will tear through your mind and eat you from the inside. Until nothing remains but me" Miranda and York rise up relieved from the pain but Davii is still toiling on the ground. He begins to calm down seconds later. "I'm fine, I just need a second. I don't know what that was" York slightly moves Davii's collar on his shirt and it is revealing he has a mysterious bite mark on his shoulder close to his neck. "Hey man when did this happen?" Davii backs away quickly. "I don't know but we gotta keep moving. Maybe what happened to us happened to everyone" York and Miranda nod in agreement. A series of moaning sounds and horrid howls can be heard in the distance. They quickly begin moving to their next destination. "Okay I have a plan guys but Im not gonna lie it can go to shit really fast" Miranda exclaims.

Davii and York inquire. “Let’s hear it, don’t hold a new idea back” York say’s. “I got a message from my dad just now telling me to head back towards the police station. There we can find him, shelter, protection and food but the catch is pretty obvious right?” Davii exhales.

“It means going back towards town with all that shit happening, We were lucky enough to even get here but we have more than we did so this might work. We have to work together though or else we might as well just dress up like the cult leaders”

York looks at davii after he finishes talking and smirks. “Dress up like cult leaders..we can dress up like the cultist and make our way through secretly. Davii remember when your dad took us on the trip for the summer and taught us how to hunt and he told us those drunk stories about him sneaking into enemy territory?" Davii gasps. "Dude your right, Do you remember our formation?" York puts his hand out. "You watch my back and I'll take the shot. We can steal some clothes and flank em. That way if we gotta pretend or kill someone. Either option can happen" York and davii shake hands and tell Miranda to follow close with davii.

"But what road should we take back? If we take the same one I really don't know if what could be back over that bridge" York says and Miranda quickly replies "Taking the highway Is what I did but there was chaos ensuing even while I crossed it. It was lucky I made it pass the ones looting cars to the grocery store when I realized what was happening" Davii seems to be staring off into space before he says “It does not matter what Is on that bridge, we are going to kill it if we see it. Its just the only way through from what Miranda is saying” They all agree but Miranda looks noticeably nervous. They begin making their way back towards where Davii and York came. They jog and maintain a fast pace. They keep going until the bridge is in sight. “There it is, I don’t hear what we heard before” Davii stops as he can hear heavy footsteps. “You guys hear that?” Miranda and York reply “No” but davii continues. “I know what im hearing, those are footsteps” but miranda ask’s him “Hey are you okay? We don’t hear anything” In the forest beside them, a strange gurgling can be heard. They freeze as the sounds startle them. They begin sprinting towards the bridge as multiple infected begin chasing them.

One of the infected grabs Yorks hood and tries to bite him before Davii shoots it in the head. They cross the bridge and the infected refuse to follow but instead retreat into the darkness again. The three begin moving forward and eventually reach the outskirts of town. "The police station is at least another mile from here" Davii says before his head begins hurting again. He visibly begins sweating as his eyes begin turning red as if the blood vessels are being torn. He begins to see symbols everywhere and his dead mother begins speaking to him. "Where were you Davii? Why couldn't you save me? Why were you not there for me Davii?" York touches his shoulder as he returns to normal. "Yeah im fine, I just think all this is getting to me. I haven't taken my medicine since this all started" York gasps. "You mean your medication that stops dementia? That's some important information davii. Are you sure your alright?" York replies. Davii says yes as they continue. They hide behind a building as multiple cultist are patrolling the city.

A young man is seen running from out of one of the stores screaming "I'm not gonna be waiting to die, fuck you guys" York immediately notices. "Dude that's Vincent" he says. One of the cultist hears him and alerts the others. He is captured by a creature and held in place. "lets see if we can get any information, maybe this will tell us what they are" Miranda says as they continue to hide and watch. A man wearing the same cloak as the others walks up. He is given a knife as he cuts off vincents clothes. Vincent begs for his life to no avail, His cries are heard by none. The cloaked man attempts to begin cutting him but stops, he drops the stake and falls to his knees. “Oh..he is here, the chosen is in the city my fellow believers. I have foreseen his ascension and I have been blessed by him to anoint thee as his humble servant” The man pulls back his head revealing he has gone blind but a third eye sits upon his forehead bleeding enough to cause two dripping rivers on his face. The rivers sit like moving tattoos on his face. The lower half of his face morphs into a gaping maw with a jagged mess of sharp teeth. He begins crying as he picks up the knife and begins chanting. He writes symbols into vincents flesh. He removes vincents tongue and ears. He removes his eyes and the creature drops him onto the ground.

As Vincent is moaning and groaning in pain his body begins convulsing violently. His skin darkening and the symbols glowing on him. His arms violently rip open exposing the skeleton, his skull splits as sharp teeth protrude from both sides. His legs elongate and also split now creating two more limbs on his lower half. The newly created creature rises and stands there blank until the cult priest looks into it with his third eye revealing the creatures glowing gold eyes. "Behold my brothers, Our master is near you see. The slaves have begun exhibiting signs of being closer to that place, the place we all will join our master to give birth to a new world" The cultist all bow as the newly transformed Vincent simply twitches looking upwards. "Ahhh you have done well priest" The creature morphs into a tall and slender man with long black twisted hair and brown skin. His eyes a beautiful and deep gold on a haunting black. The priest excitedly says “Magnificent!! I never dreamed I would be able to create a host for one of my gods Ministers, I am your humble servant. Thank you” He says as the man looks behind him and smiles. Davii begins shaking terribly as his eyes flicker between a light brown and gold. He hears in his mind “I know you hear me well vessel, let’s play a game shall we”

The environment changes entirely and only davii and the minister remain. Davii looks around to see his standing on what seems to be a black pool emanating liquid gold orbs that gently float upwards. The land around him christened with white grass and a mysterious sky. The acolyte approaches him. “You have survived, That is good. My master will enjoy taking your mind and splitting it a million different directions as he kills your world" He says with an intimidating monotone voice. "Where am I? What do you people want from me?" he asked the Minister. "What do we want from you? Isn't it obvious. You will be a host for my master and upon his ascension into godhood. You will be eviscerated from the inside and transformed into something entirely new" He begins walking away as he grabs one of the liquid orbs. "This will make it so my master can enter you more freely, You cannot stop this, no one can stop this. Your world, your reality just as had been done before will be devoured by the beast that comes for all. The enduring and terrifying emptiness that humans have feared for eternity now comes for your species. You do not understand now but I encourage you to think on what I am about to say heavily" He forces the orb into davii as small tendrils erupt from its form and begin violently attaching to Davii tearing at his skin with each pull. The minister backs away speaking in another language. "We are an immortal and powerful force and your species is a very malleable object"

York begins shaking davii as he is now immobile and he can hear an odd screeching coming from another direction and getting eerily closer. Miranda slaps davii and he wakes up. He wakes up clenching his chest and sweating profusely. The fear and confusion in his eyes causes miranda to step back suddenly. The noise now at an uncomfortable distance forces the three to retreat away from it. They go to the backdoor of a convenience store and York picks the lock. Stepping into the doorway slowly as they look around to check for anything strange, Miranda accidentally bumps into a table with a strange sludge on it. It twitches and miranda stumbles backward trying to get away from it. She bumps into York so he turns around with his weapon drawn. Davii begins hearing auditory hallucinations as he is checking the pantry for something they can quickly eat.

He grabs some vegetables and fruit and continues down a dark corridor revealing only a yellowish light at the end. York and miranda catch up and they begin walking. The creek of the pipes startles them. The darkness seemingly creeping and using deathly fingers to strangle their composure. As they walk down they finally come to the doorway where a man slamming his head against a wall repeatedly they stop and become silent. The man continues slamming his head as the sound of his skull and brain mashing against the hard cement wall reverberates through their ears. They exit the doorway and walk to the front of the store to check out the street and make sure they can leave eventually.

York opens the doors with his gun drawn. "There you see? The police station is right over the tracks. You can see the lights from the gates from here" Miranda says anxiously. They continue walking and see that the cultist have begun praying in a strange trance like state. They begin walking slowly pass them as they twitch and groan. Some of them are simply standing with their arms folded into a grotesque pose, their arms fused into their ribcage with a glassy look in their eyes. The finally come to the train tracks where the train has been toppled over about 10 yards down being hidden by the growing trees. The trees have begun emanating a gold colored dust. “What could have turned over this train?” York asked. Davii replies “It could have been one of those larger creatures but I am sure that this was a result of someone’s mind being subsumed and transformed” Miranda glances at davii surprised at the specifics of his statement. They continue down the road but multiple black vehicles are seemingly coming from behind them. They take the time to slide down the ditch next to them and wait for them to pass. Inside one of the vehicles a suspicious and deep growl is heard. “That’s towards the station! They really are still holding out” They begin running along the forest path to avoid detection on the roads.

They come to find the police station has been broken into and the cultist and multiple monsters are pouring into the buildings gates as a wave of officers pour out to meet them with the best they could find. An officer with a grenade launcher fires into the cultist blowing them apart. It is to no avail as the horde continues its march forward. Miranda's father Brandon comes up behind davii, miranda and york with a team of officers approaching after. They exclaim that they have lost the station but it was lost a day ago truly. They had ran out of food and blankets. It was only a matter of time. They tried to hold out but were rescued by a civilian named Bobby who stayed to help them get away unnoticed. Davii looks up surprised to hear the name I familiar to him but he has no memory of knowing someone with that name.

The group begins retreating deeper into the woods hoping to get away from the horde that now controls the town finally. “Hey York, I think I got something you can help me with” York looks to him with interest. When we get to Chelsea we can see if the local authorities there have also been overrun, we last spoke to them and they were hold up with the national guard trying to get sent out. They told us we had 4 hours to make it and luckily Chelsea is about 3 hours away by driving. Miranda told me before that you know something about cars right? well we had to leave an SUV about a mile west of here. If we get that SUV operational then we can probably get there on time. Davii interrupts and asks brandon an important question. “What happens if we do not make it?” Brandon pauses and he exhales heavily, there is a brief and suspenseful pause in between his words. “They..will leave us. Without a doubt” he says. As the group begin changing direction and heading west through the forest paths leading to the riverbank they overhear the sound of sobbing and what seemed to be a couple people arguing. Everyone crouches down and begins looking around, the officers with their guns drawn see a fire over a low hanging tree branch. The officers quickly run to the situation. They come across a man yelling furiously at his wife and children about an item he seems to have lost. “Who the fuck is there?!!” he screams at them while he foams at the mouth and tirelessly scratches his neck.

Brandon holds a submachine gun up to aim clearly at the man. “Just calm down alright? We’re special law enforcement, search and rescue division. “Get away? They took it, the wont admit it but they took it” he said as he began to break skin away with his scratching. ‘Took what? We cant help if you don’t tell us what is going on” The man has a noticeable twitch when he begins speaking. “They took my wish, they took my chance to ascend!!!” The officers ready their weapons and begin to look nervous. “They took my wish, they told me that if I killed the boy and the women then I could have my desire fulfilled. They said If I lead them out here and gut them both like filthy dogs that they would give me a new body to walk in. Miranda looks at the mans legs and notices theyre incredibly thin and of a dark complexion as if the limbs had been incredibly bruised and beaten. A thick concentration of blood begins coming from the mans mouth and he begins violently twitching. The man makes eye contact with davii and lunges at him like a crazed animal. The men begin firing on him but he stands nonetheless. He begins to shake and twitch as he falls to the ground seemingly having a seizure. His body begins to have a black liquid come from his eyes and mouth. The liquid has bits of gold and light in it and it releases many long tendrils that begin clamping onto the different parts of the mans face disfiguring him all the while. Davii begins hyperventilating and begins backing away. They begin shooting again but to no avail.

"Hey I don't know what the fuck is going on but we gotta get away from him" Some of the officers work to carry the woman and her child while brandon keeps firing into the man as he attempts to give York, miranda and davii time to get ahead. The man begins to have the substance pouring from every pore on his body as it latches onto different parts of his body. He begins making a sound akin to suffocation, as if he is choking violently and trying to breathe. Brandon begins sprinting in the other direction after the newly transformed man begins chasing him. He stops and begins fighting the creature with his machete. It jumps into him knocking him to the ground. It begins opening its mouth and he sticks a flash grenade into it. He shoots its leg off and runs. The grenade goes off causing a bright explosion, He keeps moving to catch up with the others

The group stops running to give brandon a chance to catch up. Miranda frozen seems to be having some sort of issue. York askes her whats wrong secretly. “I..think im losing it. Something isn't right York. I started seeing things a few hours ago but now im hearing someone or something speak to me. I don't want to turn into one of those things" She says as she begins sobbing. "Hey look around you, I already noticed two of those guys are already losing it a bit" He says referencing the other officers they are with.

Davii looks over and asks miranda, "Hey I know what you mean, I think Ive been having some crazy hallucinations myself. Its like I blank out randomly and I can hear someone talking to me and other times im in a different place entirely talking to someone I haven't met" Brandon catches up and thanks them for waiting. "Sir, I think the vehicle is just another 5 minutes to the left. I remember seeing that hanging tree right there when we first had to leave it" Brandon nods and informs everyone of their path. "Alright, everyone follow me. Keep an eye out and be ready to move when its time to move" They keep walking through the forest path and find that the vehicle is being investigated by cultist. They sit behind the bushes in the shadows of the forest.

They can overhear the cultist talking. "Whoever was in this car seems to have fled already, possibly more officers" The acolyte is interrupted by one of the priest. "It matters not, his coming is almost at hand. We must begin preparing the bodies in the town and churches immediately" They begin walking away from the vehicle as something seemingly caught their attention. The group waits for the cultist to be at a further distance before attempting to hotwire the truck. "Okay do your thing we're gonna watch your back" Brandon and the officers surround the vehicle to give York cover while he tries to turn on the truck. Davii begins to enter a daze in which he is saying the same phrase under his breath repeatedly.

"Our cold and wretched messiah, stay awake" Miranda overhears him and ask him what he is saying. Davii surprised flinches upon her putting her hand on his shoulder. "Nothing, its nothing. I just keep hearing things, words come out but it doesn't feel like I said them. I think something is wrong with me miranda. I think my hallucinations may be different from others" he says with a panicked look on his face. His teeth clenched as if his jaw and lips were locked into place. Miranda stumbles back in fear as davii seems to be losing himself. York gets the truck operational and brandon alerts the others to get inside.

Miranda begins to hold Davii's hands as he begins to settle at her touch. "We are going to make it out of this" she lays her forehead onto his and they enter the trucks backseat. As they depart and begin their journey one of the officers, "officer renton" begins to start twitching and mumbling as he sits with his eyes clothes as if he is having a nightmare.

2 hours pass and the group is almost to their destination. Officer renton has seemingly been sleep the entire time just simply mumbling under his breath. an officer "officer Bradley" ask brandon if officer renton is gonna be a liability because he is making him nervous. "Is officer renton good? This is starting to look like a liability brandon. We cant have anyone losing

their shit before we get to our destination. This is making me nervous man" Brandon reassures him that he has a plan in case any of them lose their sanity right now. "Hey miranda, York. If I lose my mind and something terrible is gonna happen if you don't stand in my way. I don't want you guys to get too caught up in our memories. End my life immediately. Something is wrong with me and I have a feeling that if we get caught by the cultist. Things will only get a lot worse for everyone else we know. If they aren't dead already" York and miranda pause with a surprised expression. "You said that completely randomly as if our reaction was suppose to be sure davii, I'll gladly kill you if you end up losing your mind. Sure that's just such a simple request to ask randomly in the back of a military truck while psychotic cultist and monsters are outside. I definitely want to think about how I might have to kill one of my best friends right now" miranda replies angrily.

York interrupts her next statement. "I got you man, Don't worry im going to protect us and you know it. Miranda I know this is tough. None of us want to hurt each other but people are losing it. We are slowly losing it. I can feel something scrapping the back of my head like rusty metal nails on chalkboard. Like something is whispering terrible dreams to me. That doesn't change the fact that we need to all be aware of whats happening and we need to be ready to do anything we need to in order to survive. To live. I have a feeling a lot of people are already doing a lot less living these days" A crude jokes forces miranda to giggle. "You have the worst sense of humor York. I know all that but your both assholes for being so mature right now. We were in high school and now look where we are. Do you think things are ever gonna go back to normal somewhere…somehow?" she asked. The truck hits an unexpected bump and officer renton attacks miranda strangling her viciously. York and davii try to pull him off but are overpowered. Brandon slams on the brakes as he crosses another bump and they are confronted by a large gate. The crazed officer renton is flung to the top of the trucks ceiling Barbwire atop the fence and bright lights flash into the trucks windshield. "Stop right where you are and state your intentions" is heard in a monotone metallic voice over a loud speaker. "Its me, brandon! I came to get passage to the evac jets. I've got my daughter and two other boys and some officers with me looking to get out of here" officer renton being held by two officers "Officers Cole and Thusia" as well as York and davii as the four begin fighting officer renton as he begins changing. Soldiers come forward from both sides of the dark road aiming at officer renton and the three against him.

Thusia tries to talk to them clearly "Hey we aren't the enemy, our friend is possessed by the madness going around, hes trying to kill this girl" Officer renton lets out a terrible screech and roar as sharp teeth push through his mouth ripping his lower jaw to pieces, his chest cavity burst open with multiple thin tentacles protruding as he lunges at the cole making a terrible gargling growl. The monstrosity that was once Officer renton begins tearing through cole with its sharp blade like appendages. The soldiers fire on him sending enough bullets to tear the rest of his mutated body to shreds. The soldiers then put handcuffs on Thusia, York, Davii and Brandon. They set the body of renton on fire with a combustion grenade and escort them through the metal gates. As they pass the gates and multiple screening devices they come across a large automatic door. One of the soldiers walks up to it and puts his eye forward. It scans his left eye and speaks "Welcome back Sgt. Benning and 10 approved guest" They enter the door and discover the evac planes are being prepared to leave a medical officer walks up to them "Okay you guys will be on evac carrier C-1, Sorry about the cuffs but as im sure you guys have noticed its better to be safe than sorry. Our detectors only detected one anomaly among you with a drone while you were 10 minutes out"

Miranda drops to her knees and the group begins sitting in place. The relief they all feel overwhelms them. As the medical officer assist them in boarding the preparations to leave commence. One by one the carriers lift into the air and begin making their way to their destination. As they fly over the town they can see the entire town is stained and different from their memories. A bright light flashes and a black sludge like liquid begins emanating from the ground and a gold beam shoots through the clouds. An incredible high pitch ring sends everyone into a state of panic as they hold their heads. York opens his eyes to see davii convulsing with his eyes glazed over with a gold tint and black liquid begins secreting from his mouth. He tries to help him but the evac carrier is soon sent out of control. They begin hurtling towards the ground, spinning violently.

A second freezes for miranda as she can see Davii with black eyes letting out a seemingly primal scream. They crash into the ground severely damaging the craft. York opens his eyes to find brandon impaled by a metal pipe. He tries to get out of his seat but is in too much pain. His leg has been decapitated and his arm is out of the socket. Miranda crawls over to him through some of the wreckage with a large head wound. She gets close enough just to touch his foot as he hangs over her body by a ripped up wires and belts. Davii walks through the now open emergency door noticeably different. York with his sight fading as he can feel his blood leaving him asks him for help. Davii speaking in two different voices in two different tones answers him. Oh you poor little creature. Your friend is gone. You are all alone and about to die. I suppose this is a just fate for something as pitiful as you. Goodbye little human.

York watches as davii walks away leaving only the sounds of manic creatures encroaching slowly. His eyes slowly begin closing as his body is now cold and his senses dulling as if he is accepting his death, he murmurs weakly saying “I guess im gonna see you kinda soon you all again after all. Im coming miranda” only the sounds of terrible creatures fill his ears.

Davii meets the cultist in the towns center. They all begin bowing as the creatures in the area all begin roaring and raising their hands to the sky. The sky begins cracking like glass as the red beam seemingly penetrates space and reality. A black figure seemingly made of a tangible liquid walks into davii as it is absorbed into him. His sclera become black with hundreds of gold symbols circulating and moving throughout his left eye, his right eye host the same but with a gold iris surrounding the pupil. His hair extends slightly and his skin now host a pale greyish tone. He snaps his fingers now donning a black suit with a gold tie that has the black liquid emanating from it slowly like a mist with droplets. He raises his hands and begins moving them as if to be opening the hole in the sky wider. He holds an orb of blue and yellow light that begins moving around in his hands. He sends into the portal and says "Our deal is now concluded Davii, it is time to bring this world into madness, strife and war. My brother has already submerged his part of this world into darkness with his vessel. He was incredibly powerful when I felt him reach into the crack that is the darkest parts of reality and pull me through. Humans have such beautiful nightmares, such lucid and fleeting sweet dreams. I see why he chose a human host" The minister forms from black mist in the air and greets his superior. My immortal and vast god Praita. To have you here before me finally is such a gift. I hope the madness I have been plaguing this species with is suiting you?" He asked but was given no answer. "You have done well but there are more important matters to tend to" Praita said with a deep and ominous voice.

"I call forth my eternal messenger, My vicious hands of a dark whisperer. My rancid teeth that rip and shred flesh from the bones of hope. My madness and grotesqueness, my anger, my burning hatred and purity. Heed my command dreadnaught" Two slender arms come through the portal in the sky. The grasp the edges of reality cracking it like glass as a horrid monster sends its head through. Six eyes on its face with no nose or mouth. The eyes arranged strangely as its other two arms help it reach further out. Its eyes move to the top of its face as a mouth opens revealing a white emptiness. Its roar, its moan was so incredibly loud. Its sadness, its madness being sung through its gaping maw. It steps completely through onto the land and raises its two top arms as if to be holding something and its bottom two arms into a prayer position. "Now march, march and spread my edict of horror onto this worlds populace"

York opens his eyes as he lays upon a sandy white beach with shining stone like trees that were of an array of colors. He gets up feeling on himself. “I’m alive? No..that wouldn’t be right. I must have passed on already” He gets up and finds a red bench. He sits on it and looks forward at a beautiful sunset that circulates an array of shades of blue, red and purple. A person walks up and sits beside him. A young woman with piercing blue eyes that seemed to house an ocean within them. Her skin a frosted white and her hair resembled an ocean of water and stars. “Do you enjoy this view York or is it okay if I call you by your real name?” The woman asked him. “I liked York, it was a nickname I came up with while me and davii were in middle school when I first came out. I have a feeling like that doesn’t matter now so call me whatever you want I guess" he said solemnly. "Well then, is there anything you wish for right now York? I am able to accomplish almost all things if only through your wish for me to do anything" The woman said to York. "I want to ask..if your god or whoever I guess well I want to see miranda. I want to tell her I'm sorry" The scenery changes to a sunrise with mixes of orange, yellow and blue forming what looked to be the ocean above. York sees miranda and goes in to hug her but she stops him. "We don't have too much time, you have to go back York, we still have a chance to save a lot of people. We will meet here again but only after you meet a man named David. He will help you come back to me" York begins sobbing and attempting to apologize for the previous events. "I..I am so sorry miranda, I promise im gonna come back, im sorry for everything" He says but miranda interrupts him. "Its okay, none of this is your fault and you did enough to help everyone keep going. Our jobs aren't done yet though, like I said. Find David. He can help you. He'll understand so to speak"

The scenery changes back to sunset. The woman appears in a beautiful black slender dress that looked like it had stars wrapped around its fabric. "Humans always have a million things they want to ask god, a million things they want to go back and change or they want to live a different life. Humans. Your creativity at these moments will never cease to amaze me" She said. Her voice like a solemn melody played by an orchestra. Beautiful, hypnotizing, melodic and comforting. "So im suppose to leave this place somehow and talk to a man named David? How will I even know how to find him?" York asked with a confused expression. "You can find him on your journey, If I tell you I fear you will not be driven to the decisions you must make. Believe my words child. It is with an aching heart I pass this task onto you and your lovely friend miranda. However. Your bond was like another I know in another world. Your journey will take your dreams and leave nothing but wonder and strife. Violence and an awakening. You must move forward my dear Jacob, Jacob Talis or else the plague, the madness, the dark and decrepit hate that took your lives will continue to spread from land to land, world to world." York is stuck in thought. "So this is deeper than I thought, I see now. Will I remember all of this after I leave here?" York asked. "You will remember this, you will also have visions of the coming future before you arrive back within your mortal form. I do hope your carry them with certainty and commitment despite this knowledge" York inhales greatly as he wakes up with his leg repaired but a large scar now present.

"So that's how this could go? Well then. I'll be back miranda. I promise" York removes the ring from mirandas corpse and lays a large fabric over her. He puts it in his pocket and begins walking through a thick forest path.

www.ingramcontent.com/pod-product-compliance
Lightning Source LLC
La Vergne TN
LVHW040958150826
845672LV00002B/747